seriously SILLY stories

Written by Laurence Anholt
Illustrated by Arthur Robins

ORCHARD BOOKS
338 Euston Road, London NW1 3BH
Orchard Books Australia
Level 17/207 Kent Street, Sydney, NSW 2000

First published in Great Britain by Orchard Books: *Snow White and the Seven Aliens* 1988, *The Emperor's Underwear* 1996 and *Billy Beast* 1996. This bind-up edition first published in 2012.

A Paperback Original

ISBN 978 1 40832 416 5

A CIP catalogue record for this book is available from the British Library.

1 3 5 7 9 10 8 6 4 2

Printed in Great Britain

Orchard Books is a division of Hachette Children's Books, an Hachette UK company.

www.hachette.co.uk

SPOT ALL THE SERIOUSLY SILLY PEOPLE!

SERIOUSLY SILLY STORYLAND

DARE TO BE BARE

Tra la-la!

★ The Fried Piper ★ Shampoozel ★ Daft Jack ★ The Emperor ★
★ Little Red Riding Wolf ★ Rumply Crumply Stinky Pin ★

Snow White dreamed of becoming a pop star. She wanted to be number one in the charts, just like her hero, Hank Hunk from Boysnog.

Snow White had a beautiful voice. She was a great dancer too. And she could even write her own songs.

Only one thing stood in her way – her wicked stepmother.

Once upon a time Snow White's
stepmother had been a famous pop star.
She had been the Mean Queen, lead singer
in The Wonderful Wicked Witches. But
now her voice was croaky and she was no
longer a star. She had become mad with
jealousy of Snow White.

"You will never be famous like me!" she would hiss. "You look too…ordinary. You don't even have a band. And besides, your nose is too small."

Then, the Mean Queen would storm
out of the room, leaving poor Snow White
to weep under the Boysnog posters in
her bedroom.

Snow White's father was a kind little man. He liked doing jigsaw puzzles and making small Plasticine models. Although he loved his daughter, he was not strong enough to stand up to his wife.

The Mean Queen had a huge dressing-room at the top of the house, with dozens of mirrors and shelves of make-up, as if she were still a great star.

11

And sometimes she forced her poor husband to sit behind the dressing-table mirror and tell her that she was still beautiful.

Mirror, mirror, on the wall,
Who has the cutest
nose of all?

From behind the mirror, her terrified husband would reply:

Mean Queen, you look a treat.
With a nose as perfect as a boiled sweet.

Then, the Mean Queen would scream with laughter and march around the house croaking her ancient songs, and remembering the day when The Wonderful Wicked Witches had appeared on the Christmas edition of Top of the Pops.

Now, Snow White often sat in the garden surrounded by little birdies and bunny rabbits, singing quietly in her beautiful clear voice. When she looked down, the Mean Queen would almost choke with rage.

Day by day, the Mean Queen could see
that Snow White was growing into a very
beautiful young woman. With that tiny
pink nose...how the Mean Queen hated her.

Only the mirror brought her comfort.

And the mirror would reply:

And so it went on. Until, one terrible night, Snow White's father could stand the lies no longer. The Mean Queen demanded:

In a tiny, trembling voice, the mirror replied:

All right. I've really had enough,
I'm fed up with the lies and stuff.
You are past it, old and sad,
Crinkly, wrinkly - really bad.
Your nose is sort of long and hairy,
Beside you, Snow White
is a Christmas fairy!

The Mean Queen leapt to her feet. With a sweep of her bony hand, she sent her make-up and bottles of perfume crashing to the floor. She seized her husband by his collar, and lifted him off his feet.

"Get Snow White OUT OF MY HOUSE," she spat into his terrified face. "Make sure she NEVER EVER returns."

The poor man crawled towards the door.
But the Mean Queen had one more order –
something so terrible that her husband
quaked in his sandals.

To prove that Snow White has really gone... BRING ME THAT TINY SNUBBY NOSE ON A COCKTAIL STICK!!!
AH, HA, HA, HAH HA HA-A-A-RRR!!!

And so, Snow White's father led his beautiful daughter far into the wild and dangerous city. With tears streaming down his face, he bought her an all-day bus pass and kissed his sweet daughter goodbye.

Of course, he could not bring himself to cut off that precious snubby nose, so he quickly modelled a false one out of some pink Plasticine which he always carried in his pocket.

This he brought back to the Mean Queen on a cocktail stick.

When the Mean Queen saw the little nose, she screamed with laughter all over again. Then she did something so ghastly that her husband felt quite ill.

She took the Plasticine nose, dipped it in mayonnaise and ATE IT, served with a side salad and French fries.

"Mmm!" she said, licking her lips. "Tasty!"

29

Meanwhile, poor Snow White wandered through the city, lost and alone.

It grew dark, and she started to feel afraid. Then, in the distance, she saw a dim green light between the buildings. Faint with hunger, she stumbled towards it and found herself in a clearing by a car park.

There in front of her was…a gleaming silver spacecraft!

A little ladder led up to a door where a flashing neon sign said:
SWINGING SPACESHIP
NIGHT CLUB.

Under this was pinned another smaller notice. This one read:

Cleaner wanted. Apply within.

31

Too tired to feel afraid, Snow White pushed the bell. Quietly, the door slid open and she stepped nervously inside.

And so it was that Snow White began her new life as a cleaner at the Swinging Spaceship Night Club. The hours were long, the pay was poor, but at least some good bands played from time to time.

"Who knows?" sighed Snow White. "Perhaps I might even hear Hank Hunk from Boysnog one day!"

One evening, Snow White was told to prepare the dressing-room for a special band who would be playing that night.

In the dressing-room she found seven identical chairs. Laid neatly on the seven identical chairs were seven identical space helmets.

I wonder who will be changing in here? she thought.

Just then, she heard strange voices singing outside in the corridor…

"Hi ho, hi ho, it's off to space we go…"

What an awful song, thought Snow White. I wonder who wrote those terrible lyrics?

The door opened and in stepped seven of the most extraordinary creatures Snow White had ever seen.

"Hi," said the first stranger. "We are the Seven Aliens. We are booked to perform tonight. We are number 4,324 in the pop charts, you know. Meet the band…"

"And what about you?" laughed Snow White, pointing at the very funny-looking alien who had spoken to her first. "What is your name?"

"He's BOTTY!" shouted all the other aliens together.

"Well," giggled Snow White. "I am very pleased to meet you. Now, if you like, I will polish your space helmets before you go on stage."

While Snow White polished, she sang a sad and beautiful song. The Seven Aliens were entranced.

"That was wonderful," gurgled Grotty when she had finished. "Tell us your name."
"I am Snow White," said Snow White.

"Oh, Snow White," sniffed Snotty. "The truth is, we cannot sing for toffee and the only words we can think of are 'hi ho, hi ho'. If you would join our band, we would blast up the charts like a rocket into space."

And so it was that Snow White and the Seven Aliens played their very first gig at the Swinging Spaceship Night Club.

Meanwhile, at home, Snow White's father wept over his lost daughter until his jigsaw puzzles were soggy. The Mean Queen, on the other hand, was in a very good mood. She went to admire herself in her magic mirror.

But to her horror the mirror replied:

I don't want to shock you, rotten Queen,
But that nose was made of Plasticine.
Snow White's nose is on her face.
She's with some blokes from outer space.

The Mean Queen turned purple. She smashed the mirror into a thousand jagged pieces.

Back at the Swinging Spaceship Night Club, Snow White and the Seven Aliens had been a huge success. A record producer had heard them play and signed them on the spot.

Snow White's dream was coming true. As Christmas approached, her single 'Snow White Alien Rap' crept higher and higher up the charts, eventually even overtaking Hank Hunk and Boysnog.

Snow White and the Seven Aliens were booked to appear on the Christmas edition of Top of the Pops.

Snow White was terribly nervous. She was sure the Mean Queen would do something to spoil her good fortune. The aliens made her promise to lock her dressing-room door and not let anyone in but them.

But with only half an hour to go before the programme, someone rattled the door handle, and a voice called...

Snow White thought the voice sounded a little strange, but she just had to see if it was really Hank Hunk from Boysnog come to see her!

She opened the door a tiny crack.
In burst a tall figure with blonde hair.
It looked like Hank Hunk… But surely
there was something strange about his nose?

Alas! It was the Mean Queen.

When the aliens came to collect Snow White they found her completely frozen with stage fright. No matter how much they tried to reassure her, she simply could not move her arms and legs, let alone dance or sing.

In despair, they carried her, like a statue, out of the dressing-room and laid her gently on the stage.

"It's no use," bawled Botty. "We'll have to sing 'hi ho, hi ho…'"

51

The programme started.

"FAN-TABULOUS Christmas Greetings, pop fans," called the announcer. "We've got a SEN-SATIONAL seasonal line up for you, including the incredible new discovery, Snow White and those Seven EXTREMELY STRANGE Aliens. We've also got Hank Hunk and Boysnog, and later…"

Snow White was still unable to move. To the Seven Aliens, it seemed like a hundred years passed by. Then, at the back of the studio, someone began to push his way through the crowd.

"Let me through," he said. "I'm a qualified heart-throb. I simply must see her."

It was Hank Hunk! This time it really was
him. Snow White's heart began to flutter.

"Oh, Snow White," whispered Hank, "please sing. Sing for me." He bent towards Snow White. A long blonde curl fell across one eye. Gently, he kissed her lips.

Snow White leapt to her feet.

"OK BOYS. Let's GROO-VE!" she shouted.

Snow White and the Seven Aliens leapt into the spotlight and began to play. Across the nation, every family threw down their Christmas crackers and began gyrating to the fantastic sounds on TV.

Everybody, except one person. High in her dark dressing-room, the Mean Queen stared into her shattered mirror and muttered:

Mirror, mirror, smashed to bits,

Today I really feel...the PITS!

But her husband, jiving in front of the
TV, called up to her:

That's funny, honey, I feel quite perky,
Come downstairs and have some turkey.
If you're good, you never know,
I might get out the mistletoe.

On New Year's Eve, there were seven special guests at Hank and Snow White's wedding. Their names were Scotty, Spotty, Dotty, Snotty, Potty, Grotty and Botty.

And they all blasted off for a honeymoon in the stars.

"Hi ho, hi ho…"

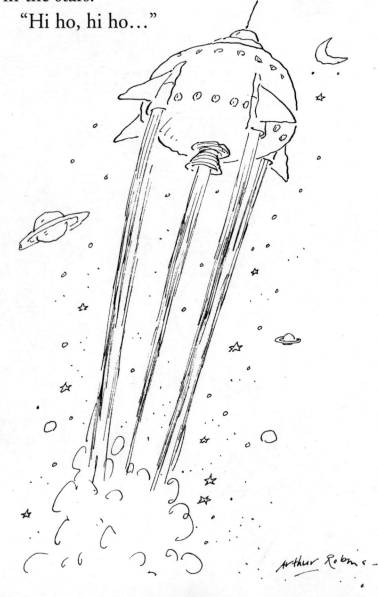

THE EMPEROR'S
UNDERWEAR

There was once a country where no one wore any clothes at all.

It was a very sensible thing to do. There was no washing, no ironing, no mending, no folding, no putting away, no dressing or undressing.

So there was plenty of time for really
important things, like climbing trees and
doing handstands and dancing about in the
sunshine.

All through the summer it was the happiest country in the world. Without their clothes, everyone was treated alike – big or small, rich or poor.

Even the Emperor was just like an ordinary person, without a crown or fancy clothes.

In fact, people spent most of the day
laughing out loud, because everything
seemed so funny.

After all, even strict Headmasters aren't very frightening in their birthday suits.

Of course, there were no uniforms either. So when the police chased the robbers it was hard to tell one from the other. They all got into such a muddle that they just fell about laughing.

There was no doubt about it – in summer, it was the happiest country in the world. But in winter . . .

. . . that was a different story all together.
All through the winter, the icy north wind
whistled around the streets until every bare
botty turned blue with cold.

One particularly chilly morning, the Emperor woke up with goose pimples all over his royal body. The wind moaned around the palace . . .

. . . and the Emperor moaned around the palace, too.

He jumped up and down and rubbed his hands together, but by breakfast time even his goose pimples had goose pimples.

All morning the snow fell, and throughout the land people stayed indoors and shivered like blueberry jellies.

Then, at lunch time, there was a knock at the palace door. In came two strange men.

The Emperor could see straight away that
they had come from a different country
because they were wearing CLOTHES! But
being a kind Emperor, he tried not to laugh.

"Good day, Your Noble Nakedness," said the first man, stamping the snow from his boots.

"Greetings, Oh Royal Rudeness," said
the second man, brushing the ice from his
woollen hat.

"We are tailors from a distant nation,"
they said.

The Emperor wasn't sure what a tailor was,
but he smiled and shivered politely.

"We have come to make you the most
beautiful bloomers in the world to keep
your royal bottom warm," they announced.

"What?" said the Emperor. "Me? Wear knickers? You must be joking. I have to set an example to my people, you know."

"Yes, yes, Your Beautiful Bareness, but these are not ordinary pantaloons, they are MAGIC KNICKERBOCKERS, because they will be completely INVISIBLE to the naked eye (if you'll pardon the pun).

No one will be able to see them at all – unless they are a complete banana brain, that is!"

"Amazing!" said the Emperor, his teeth
chattering a bit more.

"Mind you," continued the tailors, "magic undies don't come cheap. You will have to start us an Underwear Account at the bank so that we can buy all the magic wool we need."

So the tailors moved into the palace. Night and day, and day and night, they cut and stitched and sewed and made, not one pair of underwear, but hundreds and thousands of pairs in every shape and size.

There were Y-Fronts and Y-Not Fronts, and Boxer Shorts and Thermal Long-Johns and Purple Posing Pouches and Itsy Bitsy Teeny Weeny Yellow Polka Dot Bikinis and Woolly Winter Warmers and even Leopard Skin Tonga Thongs.

Of course, the Emperor and everyone at the palace could see *exactly* what they were doing, but no one said a word in case people thought that *they* were complete banana brains.

At last the tailors brought the Emperor
a pair of Y-Fronts and a woolly vest, all
extra large size.

The Emperor allowed the tailors to help him squeeze into them.

"Oooh!" he said, "They're all nice and warm – even though I can't see them!"

The Emperor was so pleased with his
new underwear, he hopped onto his bicycle
and went for a ride around the town.

When he had gone, the tailors began to laugh and rub their wicked hands together, "Snee hee heee!"

The Emperor rode proudly backwards and forwards along the High Street and although it was still snowing, a large crowd gathered to watch.

Of course, everyone could see the royal underwear perfectly well, but they didn't want anyone to think that *they* were silly old banana brains, so they said nothing at all; only clapped and cheered as the Emperor pedalled by.

All of a sudden, a tiny boy who was shivering on his father's shoulders pointed his little cold finger at the Emperor and shouted:

"Shh!" hissed his father. "That's the Emperor, and he's not wearing anything!"

"Oh yes, he is!" shouted the boy. "Dat man wearing nice warm woolly panties. Me want some woolly panties too!"

"The Emperor is wearing panties,"
someone whispered. "The Emperor's
wearing underwear!"

"Yes!" everyone shouted. "The Emperor's wearing underwear and WE WANT SOME TOO!"

The Emperor turned all red inside his white woollies and pedalled back to the palace.

"I really am a big banana brain," he sighed. "Whatever have I started?"

In no time all, the wicked tailors opened a big underwear shop in the High Street and people soon began queuing outside.

It wasn't long before everyone started wearing underwear. Some people wore socks too . . .

. . . and trousers and shirts, and even ties on Sundays.

And of course, it wasn't long before they had to spend all their time washing . . .

. . . and ironing . . .

. . . and putting away.

Although the people weren't cold anymore, they didn't laugh quite so often. Policemen looked like policemen, teachers looked like teachers. . .

. . . and the Emperor looked so important in his royal clothes that nobody spoke to him anymore. He began to feel very lonely and fed up.

One hot day, in the middle of summer, when everyone was sweltering in their woollen clothes, the Emperor decided he had had enough.

He pulled off his royal robes and his crown and hopped back onto his bicycle.

Then he rode proudly up and down the High Street carrying a large sign. It said . . .

And on the back it said. . .

All the people turned out to clap and cheer.
Then they began to pull their clothes off
too!

The wicked tailors sat in their shop and got hotter and hotter and more miserable. No one was interested in buying anything.

In no time at all everyone was laughing
again – just as they had before.

Soon even the tailors joined in. They set up a stall selling suntan lotion and ice lollies instead.

But the person who laughed loudest of all was the Emperor himself.

"Perhaps I am a banana brain," he chuckled, "But I'm a big, bare, happy, old banana brain!"

And he cycled away into the sunshine.

BILLY BEAST

Betty and Benjamin Beast were very proud of their castle.

They thought it was the most wonderful building for miles around. It had taken them years to get it just right with lovely green mouldy walls and black puddles in the corridors.

There were damp, dark bedrooms with snails on the pillows and smelly cellars too.

At weekends, you would always find Benjamin up a stepladder whistling happily as he hung new cobwebs in corners or painted fresh mud on the ceilings.

And when their beastly friends came for dinner, it was hard not to show off the new kitchen with its sweet little scampering cockroaches in all the cupboards, and hot and cold running slime in the taps.

There was only one thing that Betty and Benjamin were more proud of than their home, and that was their fine young son, Billy Beast.

They loved Billy more than words can say and the truth is, Billy was a bit spoiled.

They were always giving him some little treat or other – an enormous pet toad in a box, or as much crunchy earwig ice-cream as a beastly boy could eat, which wasn't very good for him.

Billy always had the best of everything – even private belching lessons after Beastie School.

By the time he was sixteen Billy had grown into a fine looking beast. He was tall and strong with plenty of fleas in his hair and the sharpest, brown teeth a beast could wish for.

The truth was, there wasn't a girl beast around who wasn't in love with young Billy, with those twinkling yellow eyes and that cute way he had of wiping his snout with the hairs on the back of his hand – who could resist?

But as far as Benjamin and Betty were concerned, it would have to be a very special girl beast who could be disgusting enough to marry their son.

So the three of them just carried on living happily together from day to day.

Billy and his toad practised their burping and everyone who met the Beast family thought they were the luckiest, smelliest, most horribly beautiful family they had ever met.

Then one morning, Benjamin and Betty went out gathering frogspawn for lunch, leaving young Billy playing quietly with his toad in his bedroom.

Billy heard a noise outside and when he looked out of his window he saw an old man wandering about in their beautiful weedy garden. He had tied his horse to the tree and he was busy STEALING BETTY'S PRIZE WINNING PRICKLY ROSES!

"Hoi! What do you think you're doing?" shouted Billy. "This is a private castle, you know. My mum will eat you if she catches you here."

When the man looked up at the castle and saw young Billy Beast all hairy and horrid with a big toad sitting on his head he was absolutely TERRIFIED.

"Oh p-please don't eat me, Mr Beast," he stammered. "I got lost and . . . and I promised my beautiful daughter I would bring her a red rose and . . ."

"Well not from our garden, pal!" snorted Billy.

The man was so frightened, he promised that he would send his daughter, Beauty, to marry Billy if he was allowed to go free.

"All right," Billy agreed, "but she'd better come soon or my dad will be after you too."

"I . . . I'll send her straight away," said the poor man, jumping onto his horse.

"And she'd better be as beautiful as you say," Billy called after him.

"Oh yes, oh yes she is," shouted the man riding away as fast as he could. "There's nothing in the world more beautiful than my daughter."

"What? More beautiful than my toad?" called Billy. But the man was already out of sight.

When Betty and Benjamin came home, Bill told them the whole story. "I'm going to be married," he grunted happily, "to the most beautiful girl in the world – the man said there's nothing in the world more beautiful than Beauty."

Betty and Benjamin were very pleased to think of their son married to the most beautiful girl in the world, although they found it hard to believe that anyone could be quite as good looking as their Billy.

Early next morning, Beauty arrived. Billy saw her horse coming up the hill towards the castle.

He quickly ran to the mirror to make
sure his teeth were nice and black and he
checked that his breath was good and
smelly. He splashed a little skunk juice
under his arms – then he ran to the door to
meet his bride.

Billy was very excited. As the doorbell rang, he twisted his face into the most beautifully disgusting shape that he could manage, then pulled open the door.

When Beauty saw Billy, she almost
fainted on the spot. Billy could understand
that, because his handsome looks often
made girls feel weak at the knees.

What he couldn't understand was that Beauty wasn't beautiful! In fact she looked just like an ordinary GIRL!

She was hardly hairy at all, except on her head. And her TEETH – they were all sort of white and shiny!

She had a horrid pink NOSE where her
snout should be and little FINGERS instead
of nice claws. UGH! It was DISGUSTING!

"I bet she hasn't even got a hairy chest,"
thought Billy in dismay.

Betty and Benjamin were also disappointed, but they tried not to show it. The poor girl had come a long way to marry their son and she seemed upset too.

"I'm sure she will look better once we get rid of that nasty white dress and pop her into a nice sloppy mud bath," said Betty kindly.

"And she'll probably get hairier as she gets older," suggested Benjamin. "Perhaps she hasn't been eating a healthy diet – I expect she's hungry now after that long journey. Let's start her off with a lovely bowl of warm earwax and slug juice."

So Betty and Benjamin set about trying to make Beauty a little more beastly, and Billy went into the garden with his toad and sulked.

After a few days, Beauty began to get used to living with the Beasts, and Billy had to admit that she was looking a little better; at least she was getting more smelly.

But then Beauty would go and spoil it all by doing something revolting like washing her hands before a meal or combing her hair and everyone realised that no matter how they tried, Beauty would never be truly disgusting.

Billy promised his parents that he would try to get along with her, although he swore he would never marry her. He patiently taught her to burp nicely and to dribble, but she was slow to learn.

Then, one morning in the garden, something HORRID happened. Billy had just allowed Beauty to play with his toad when she turned around and TRIED TO KISS HIM!

With those white teeth and rosy lips, it almost made poor Billy sick just thinking about it! He wiped his mouth and jumped away.

Beauty began to cry, "I can't help it!" she wailed. "I can't help looking like this. Of course I would like to be hairy and horrid like you. But couldn't you try to love me for what I am instead of the way I look."

Billy was really a kind-hearted beast. He began to feel sorry for Beauty. He saw that she was right. It doesn't really matter what you look like, it is the person inside that counts.

Before he knew what he was doing, Billy had put down his toad and taken Beauty into his hairy arms, he put his snout close to her little head and ... SMACK! He kissed her tiny snubby nose.

Right before Billy's yellow eyes, Beauty began to change! She grew hairier and hairier. Her teeth grew brown and longer. Her fingers turned into beautiful claws!

At last she stood before him – a truly
wonderful beastie girl with the most
gorgeous damp snout Billy had ever seen
and a delightful smell of old socks and
kangaroo sweat.

Beauty explained that the man who had stolen the roses was not her father, but a wicked wizard who had cast a spell on her.

She would lose her beastly looks until the day someone like Billy was kind enough to kiss her and break the spell.

Billy was so happy, he didn't know what to say. He just dribbled a little. And the beastly couple skipped happily up the steps of the castle, claw in claw, burping excitedly to each other.

And they were all disgustingly happy for
the rest of their beastly lives.

Billy Bonkers

'Utterly bonkers!
A riot of fun! I loved it!'
– Harry Enfield

**Mad stuff happens with Billy Bonkers!
Whether he's flying through the air propelled
by porridge power, or blasting headfirst into a
chocolate-covered planet – life is never boring
with Billy, it's BONKERS!**

**Three hilarious stories in one from an award-
winning author and illustrator team.**

978 1 84616 151 3 £4.99 pbk   978 1 40830 357 3 £5.99 pbk   978 1 40831 465 4 £4.99 pbk

Max and Molly's Guide To Trouble!

Meet Max and Molly: terrorising the neighbourhood really extremely politely...

Max and Molly's guides guarantee brilliantly funny mayhem and mischief as we learn how to be a genius, catch a criminal, build an abominable snowman and stop a Viking invasion!

978 1 40830 519 5 £4.99 Pbk
978 1 40831 572 9 eBook

978 1 40830 520 1 £4.99 Pbk
978 1 40831 573 6 eBook

978 1 40830 521 8 £4.99 Pbk
978 1 408 31574 3 eBook

978 1 40830 522 5 £4.99 Pbk
978 1 408 31575 0 eBook